Think You Can

Eleanor Robins

High Noon Books
Novato, California

Cover Design: Jill Zwicky
Interior Illustrations: Rick Hackney

International Standard Book Number: 1-57128-183-5

9 8 7 6 5 4 3 2 1 0
0 9 8 7 6 5 4 3 2 1

Contents

CHAPTER 1

Stay After Class

Dave was ready to go. He looked at the clock. He could hardly wait to get out of math class.

The bell rang. Dave got up from his desk. He was always the first one out of class. And he always tried to be the last one to get to class.

"Dave, stay after class. I need to see you," Mr. Green said. Mr. Green was Dave's math teacher.

Dave wanted to run out the door. But he couldn't do that. He had to stay.

Jill got up from her desk. She sat next to Dave. She always made good grades in math.

Jill smiled at Dave. Then she said, "See you in our next class."

Jill was also in Dave's science class. She sat next to Dave in that class, too. Sometimes she asked him for help with her science classwork.

Mr. Green said, "Come back to my desk with me, Dave."

Mr. Green's desk was in the back of the room. He always talked to students next to his desk. That way the other students could not hear what he said.

"Why did I have to stay?" Dave asked.

But Dave knew why.

"We need to talk about your paper. The one you turned in yesterday," Mr. Green said.

"What about it?" Dave asked. But he knew. He had done a bad job on the paper.

"Most of your answers are wrong. Did you try to do well on this, Dave? Or did you just put down anything for an answer?" Mr. Green asked.

"Sure I tried," Dave said.

The math had been hard. He didn't know how to do it.

"I think you have quit trying, Dave," Mr. Green said.

"No, I haven't," Dave said.

Dave was getting mad. He didn't want to hear anything more about his math.

Mr. Green had more to say. "I know you can do better than this, Dave."

Dave didn't say anything. He knew he couldn't do any better.

Mr. Green said, "Do you need some extra help? Stay after school one afternoon. I can help you then."

Dave looked across the room. He saw his best friend Mike. Mike was in the next class.

Mike was looking at Dave. He had a worried look on his face. The other students were looking at Dave, too.

Dave knew Mike was worried about him.

The students couldn't hear what Mr. Green was saying. But they could tell it was about

Dave's math grade.

Dave didn't want them to know he needed extra help.

Dave said, "I don't need extra help. I need to go. I can't be late to my next class."

"OK, Dave. But think about what I said," Mr. Green said.

Dave started to hurry out of the room.

Mr. Green said, "Wait, Dave. I'll give you a late pass."

Dave didn't wait. He walked even faster. He didn't care about the pass. He just wanted to get out of that class.

CHAPTER 2

Almost Late

Dave almost ran down the hall to his science class. He couldn't be late. Or he would have to miss wrestling practice.

Dave started into his class. Just then the late bell started to ring.

He went quickly to his desk. He sat down just as the bell stopped ringing.

"Do you have a late pass, Dave?" Mrs. Lake asked. Mrs. Lake was his science teacher.

"No," Dave said.

Students were almost never late to Mrs. Lake's class.

Mrs. Lake said, "Watch the time, Dave. A few more seconds, and you would have been late. Then you would have had to stay in study hall tomorrow."

Mrs. Lake always gave study hall to late students. They had to study their science for 30 minutes after school. She would help them with science work. Or they could work on their own.

"You get to answer the first homework question, Dave," Mrs. Lake said.

She had called on him because he was almost late.

But Dave didn't care. Science was his best

class. He always had his homework.

Dave quickly got out his homework. The other students were ready to check their homework, too. They checked all of the homework. Dave made 100 on his.

Then Mrs. Lake said, "Time for our lab work. Get a partner."

Quickly Jill asked, "Dave, will you be my partner again?"

"Sure," Dave said.

Jill had a hard time in science. Dave did most of the work when he and Jill worked together. He didn't mind. He liked to be Jill's partner.

They walked over to a lab table.

They worked quietly for a few minutes.

Then Jill said, "You are really good at science."

Dave didn't know what to say. So he didn't say anything.

Then slowly Jill said, "I'm good at math. I make good grades in math."

Dave still didn't say anything. He didn't want to talk about math. He didn't even want to think about math.

Then slowly Jill said, "You are so nice to help me with science. I'll be glad to help you with your math."

"I don't need any help with math," Dave said. He didn't mean to say it so loudly.

"I'm sorry, Dave. I didn't mean to make you mad," Jill said.

"You didn't make me mad. Just keep your mind on science. Then maybe you'll do better in this class. And you won't need my help," Dave said.

Jill had a hurt look on her face.

Dave felt bad about what he had said. He was sorry he had upset Jill.

Dave liked science. But he was glad when the science class was over.

CHAPTER 3

Six Points

Dave was glad when school was over for the day. He was glad he had a match that afternoon.

Wrestling was hard work. But it made him feel good. He was always glad to wrestle someone from another school.

Dave hurried to the wrestling room. Mike was already there.

Dave was ready to wrestle. First, he had to get weighed. He got in line behind Mike.

"What did Mr. Green want? Did you get a

bad grade on your math paper?" Mike asked.

"Yeah. But I don't want to talk about it," Dave said.

"OK. We'll talk about wrestling. I wish I could win my match today," Mike said.

Dave said, "You've been working hard. So maybe you'll win."

"Maybe. A win would be great. But I just hope I don't get beaten so badly this time," Mike said.

Dave said, "Remember what the coach always says. Think you can't do it. And you won't be able to do it. Think you can do it. And maybe you can do it."

Mike said, "I know. Maybe I can this time."

Dave was glad when they were weighed. He and Mike had not added any weight. They would not have to sit the match out. They could wrestle in their weight classes.

They were both ready for their matches to start. But first both teams had to do practice exercises. Then they had to shake hands with the other team.

Dave shook hands with the boy he was to wrestle. The boy frowned at Dave. Dave frowned at the boy.

Mike wrestled first. He wasn't able to pin the boy. But he did win on points.

Dave could hardly wait for his match to start. He had beaten the boy three times before. The boy had never beaten him.

Dave got the first takedown. But the boy was able to escape. In the second period Dave was able to pin him.

Dave added six points to the score for his team. That made him feel very good.

It had been an easy match for him. His next match would not be easy. Saturday he would have to wrestle Big Tom.

Dave had lost most of his matches his first year on the team. Yet he had learned a lot from every match he lost.

The last two years only one boy had beaten him. Big Tom. Big Tom had beaten him every time they had wrestled.

In the second period, Dave
was able to pin him.

Big Tom wasn't big in size. But no one had ever beaten him. That was why he was called Big Tom.

Big Tom had been able to pin everyone. Most of his pins were in the first period. He had never had to wrestle in more than two periods.

Dave was going to work very hard before his next match. He hoped to be ready for Big Tom.

CHAPTER 4

After Class Again

Dave wasn't ready for his math class the next morning.

Dave was the last one to get to class. He hoped to be the first one out of class. The late bell rang just as he sat down.

Mr. Green said, "Get out your homework. You can check your own papers today."

All the other students got out their homework. Dave didn't have anything to get out.

Mr. Green looked around the room.

"Dave, where is your homework paper?" Mr. Green had a frown on his face.

Dave said, "I had a wrestling match after school yesterday. I didn't have much time to do it after the match."

Dave did have time to do it. He just didn't want to do it. Why do it? Most of his answers would have been wrong. So he hadn't done it.

He wasn't going to tell Mr. Green that. He didn't want his classmates to know he couldn't do the math.

"See me after class," Mr. Green said. He seemed to frown even more.

So much for being the first one out of class!

Dave thought the class would never end.

And he had to stay late on top of that.

The bell rang.

Dave got up to go. Maybe Mr. Green had forgotten he had told him to stay.

"Come back to my desk, Dave," Mr. Green said.

Dave saw Mike walk in the door. Mike saw Dave. Mike got a worried look on his face.

Dave walked back to Mr. Green's desk.

Mr. Green said, "I want you to do well in this class, Dave. I'm always willing to help you after school."

"I don't need any help. I just didn't have time to do my homework," Dave said.

"That excuse doesn't work for me, Dave.

Your math class should come before your wrestling," Mr. Green said.

Dave started to get mad. He couldn't help it that he didn't know how to do his math.

Math had always been hard for him. But he wasn't going to tell Mr. Green that.

Mr. Green said, "You know how Coach Parker feels about students who don't do their schoolwork. I have to tell him about this."

That was just what Dave needed. Now Coach Parker would give him a hard time about his math, too.

CHAPTER 5

Almost Late Again

Dave was almost late to science class again.

Mrs. Lake said, "You just made it again today, Dave."

Dave didn't say anything. He got out his homework. The other students had already taken their homework out.

"Dave, you can answer the first homework question for us," Mrs. Lake said.

For the second day in a row Dave made 100 on his science homework.

Then Mrs. Lake told them it was time to pick a lab partner. Jill quickly turned to a girl near her. She asked the girl to be her partner.

Dave could tell Jill was still upset with him. Dave liked Jill. He wished he hadn't upset her the day before.

One of the wrestlers asked Dave to be his lab partner.

Lab time was OK. But is was more fun to do the lab work with Jill.

After school was over, Dave hurried to the wrestling room. Mike was already there. He was in line to be weighed.

Mike moved to the back of the line when he saw Dave.

"What's going on? Why did Mr. Green keep you after class?" Mike asked.

"I didn't do my homework," Dave said.

"Why? Didn't you know how to do it?" Mike asked.

"I didn't want to do it," Dave said.

Mike looked surprised. "Did you tell Mr. Green that?"

Dave said, "No, I told him I didn't have time to do it. I told him I had a wrestling match."

Mike looked even more surprised. "You really told him that?"

"Yeah," Dave answered.

"You better hope Coach Parker doesn't find out you said that," Mike said.

Dave said, "No such luck. Mr. Green said he was going to tell Coach Parker."

"Then he will do it just as soon as he sees him. Coach Parker isn't going to like it," Mike said.

Dave didn't say anything. He knew Coach Parker wasn't going to like what he had said to Mr. Green. He wished Mike would quit talking about it.

Mike had more to say. "You know how Coach Parker feels about schoolwork. He might make you drop off the team. Or sit out the next match," Mike said.

"I can't sit out the next match. I have to wrestle Big Tom," Dave said.

Mike said, "Maybe. But you know how Coach Parker feels about students who don't do their work."

Dave started to get mad. He said, "I know it. You don't have to keep telling me."

Dave was glad that it was Mike's turn to be weighed. Then he couldn't say any more to him about his math.

Dave worked hard at practice. He did a few more stretching exercises than anyone else. He did more sit-ups then anyone else. He did more push-ups than anyone else. He ran one lap more around the school than anyone else.

Then he worked on his takedowns with Mike. Next he worked on his escapes with Mike.

Dave was tired. But he worked as hard as he could. He wanted to be in better shape than Big Tom.

Coach Parker called over to Dave. "Stop for a few minutes, Dave. We need to talk."

Dave didn't think Mr. Green had had time to talk to Coach Parker. But he must have talked to him. Why else would Coach Parker want to see him?

CHAPTER 6

Extra Help?

Coach Parker said, "You have been working very hard, Dave. I think you can beat Big Tom at the match on Saturday."

Dave was surprised. He said, "I just hope I can last all three periods with him. I have never made it to the third period. He always pins me before then."

"Will his past wins make points against you in your next match?" Coach Parker asked.

"No," Dave answered.

Dave didn't know why Coach Parker had asked him that question. Coach Parker knew that the answer was no.

"Then don't think about what Big Tom has done in the past. Think only about your next match with him," Coach Parker said.

Dave didn't think he would be able to do that. He couldn't forget the times Big Tom had beaten him. In some of the matches Big Tom had pinned him in the first period.

Coach Parker said, "Dave, you work hard. You're in good shape. You're smart. You can beat Big Tom."

Dave was glad Coach Parker thought he could beat Big Tom. But he didn't think he could.

"You can beat Big Tom, Dave."

Coach Parker said again, "You can beat him. Dave."

"But how? He's stronger than I am," Dave said.

"Big Tom has never had to wrestle more than two periods," Coach Parker said.

Dave knew he was right. Big Tom always pinned the other wrestlers before the end of period two.

Coach Parker said, "I don't think Big Tom is in shape to wrestle all three periods."

Dave had never thought about that.

"Make him wrestle three periods. And I think you will beat him," Coach Parker said.

Dave thought about what the coach had said.

Maybe the coach was right. Maybe he could beat Big Tom.

"Stay after practice. I'll give you some extra help," Coach Parker said.

He had to work hard before Saturday. He had to last all three periods with Big Tom. Just going all three periods might not be a win for him. But it would be almost like a win.

CHAPTER 7

We Need to Talk

The next morning seemed to pass quickly. Soon it was time for lunch.

Dave met Mike in the lunchroom. They looked for a place to sit.

Coach Parker called to Dave. He said, "Dave, we need to talk. Bring your tray over here."

Dave was sure that Mr. Green had talked to the coach. He could tell it from the way Coach Parker looked.

"See you later," Dave said to Mike. He knew Coach Parker didn't want anyone else to sit with them.

Dave walked slowly over to where Coach Parker sat. He put his tray on the table and then sat down.

Coach Parker said, "What's this about you not doing your math homework? That you didn't have time to do it because you had to wrestle?"

Dave didn't know what to say. So he didn't say anything.

"Mr. Green thinks you may not know how to do the math. He thinks that may be why you didn't do it," Coach Parker said.

He waited for Dave to say something.

He said, "I don't need Mr. Green's help. I wouldn't have time to stay after school. I need to work out as much as I can."

"You know how I feel about schoolwork, Dave. You have to make time to do it. And to get extra help when you need it. So you might have to quit the wrestling team," Coach Parker said.

Dave said, "But I have to wrestle Big Tom on Saturday."

"You don't have to wrestle anyone. Your schoolwork comes first. You told Mr. Green you didn't have time to do your homework. Then you don't have time to wrestle," Coach Parker said.

Dave just sat there. He didn't know what to say.

Then Coach Parker said, "Think about what I said, Dave. Make extra time to do your homework. Or to get the extra help you need. Do that or else you won't be on my team."

Coach Parker got up from the table.

"Work things out with Mr. Green. Do it before Saturday, Dave," Coach Parker said.

Dave wasn't sure he could do that.

Coach Parker said, "Think about what I said, Dave. I don't want to have to put you off the team."

Dave watched Coach Parker go out of the lunchroom.

Dave was always willing to work hard in wrestling. It made him a better wrestler. But it was easy to work hard when he did well.

He didn't want to work harder in math. It wouldn't do him any good to work harder. Math wasn't the same as wrestling.

What was he going to do? He couldn't get put off the wrestling team.

CHAPTER 8

Think You Can

Dave thought things over. He knew what he had to do. After school he went to see Mr. Green. He told Mr. Green he would stay for extra help. He said he would do all the homework he had not done.

Mr. Green talked to Coach Parker again.

Then Coach Parker talked to Dave. "You can stay on the team as long as you do all your work."

Dave could wrestle Big Tom on Saturday.

Dave could hardly wait.

Then Saturday came. It was time for his match with Big Tom to begin.

Dave looked over at Big Tom. Big Tom wasn't really big. He weighed only a pound more than Dave did.

Dave couldn't let Big Tom pin him in the first or second period. He had to make it to the third period.

It was time for Dave to shake hands with Big Tom. Big Tom always looked as mean as he could. He tried to scare the other wrestlers.

Dave shook hands with Big Tom. Then he walked over to Coach Parker.

Coach Parker said, "Think about what we talked about, Dave. You're in good shape. And

Dave shook hands with Big Tom.

you're smart. You can beat Big Tom."

"But he has never lost to anyone," Dave said.

"You can't think about what he did in the past. Forget he is Big Tom. Just think about what you know how to do," Coach Parker said.

Dave would try to do that. It would not be easy.

Coach Parker patted him on the back. He said, "Big Tom may always get the first takedown. But don't let that upset you. You can still beat him."

Big Tom always got the first takedown.

"Remember what I always say, Dave. Think you can't do it. Then you won't be able to do it. Think you can do it. Then maybe you can."

"I'll do my best, Coach," Dave said.

"That's all you have to do, Dave. Just your best," Coach Parker said.

The first period began.

Big Tom dove at Dave's right leg. He easily got the first takedown. Dave was able to escape. That made him feel better about the takedown.

The first period was over. And Big Tom had not pinned Dave. But Big Tom was winning in points.

The second period seemed to take forever. But it wasn't any longer than the first. Dave didn't get pinned. But he was behind badly in points.

Dave felt very tired. Every muscle in his

body seemed to hurt. Dave wished he could quit. But he never had quit. He wasn't going to quit now.

Less than twenty seconds were left in the match. He heard Coach Parker's voice.

Coach Parker said, "Dave, you are behind badly in points. But you can still win. Just think you can. And pin him to the mat."

Dave wouldn't give up. He would give it his best. Maybe he could pin Big Tom.

Dave got Big Tom down on the mat. Big Tom was not able to escape. Dave did it. He was able to pin Big Tom.

Dave had won. He had beaten Big Tom.

Every muscle in his body seemed to hurt.

Still, he felt good.

It had not been easy for Dave to beat Big Tom. He thought he could do it. And he did.

Coach Parker patted Dave on the back. He said, "You did it, Dave. All your hard work paid off for you."

Coach Parker was right. All of Dave's hard work had paid off. But it was easy to work hard when it helped him do well in something he liked. Would hard work help him pass his math, too?

Dave didn't know. It wasn't going to be easy to work hard when it didn't seem to help his grade.

Well, he would get help from Mr. Green after school. He would even ask Jill for some help.

Maybe with hard work and extra help he could pass math. It would not be easy. But now he was ready to give it his best.